HOW THE GRINCH STOLE CHRISTMAS

A 50TH-ANNIVERSARY RETROSPECTIVE

BY Dr. Seuss

With 32 pages of rarely seen Seuss images and commentary by CHARLES D. COHEN

RANDOM HOUSE • NEW YORK

Published in the United States by Random House Children's Books, a division of Random House, Inc., New York. *How the Grinch Stole Christmas!* originally published in a different form by Random House, Inc., in 1957. 50th-Anniversary Edition published in 2007.

RANDOM HOUSE and colophon are registered trademarks of Random House, Inc.

www.randomhouse.com/kids
www.seussville.com

Educators and librarians, for a variety of teaching tools, visit us at www.randomhouse.com/teachers

Library of Congress Cataloging-in-Publication Data
Seuss, Dr.
How the Grinch stole Christmas! / by Dr. Seuss ;
a 50th anniversary retrospective with 32 pages of rarely seen Seuss images, and commentary by Charles D. Cohen. — 50th anniversary ed.
    p. cm.
SUMMARY: The Grinch tries to stop Christmas from arriving by stealing all the presents and food from the village, but much to his surprise it comes anyway.
Includes commentary and notes about the author and the story.
Includes bibliographical references.
ISBN: 978-0-375-83847-7 (trade) — ISBN: 978-0-375-93847-4 (lib. bdg.)
[1. Christmas—Fiction. 2. Stories in rhyme.] I. Cohen, Charles D. II. Title.
PZ8.3.G276Hq 2007 [E]—dc22   2006027026

Printed in the United States of America   10 9 8 7 6 5 4 3   50th Anniversary Edition

Illustration credits can be found on page 85.

CONTENTS

How The GRINCH STOLE CHRISTMAS

For Teddy Owens

E very *Who*
Down in *Who*-ville
Liked Christmas a lot . . .

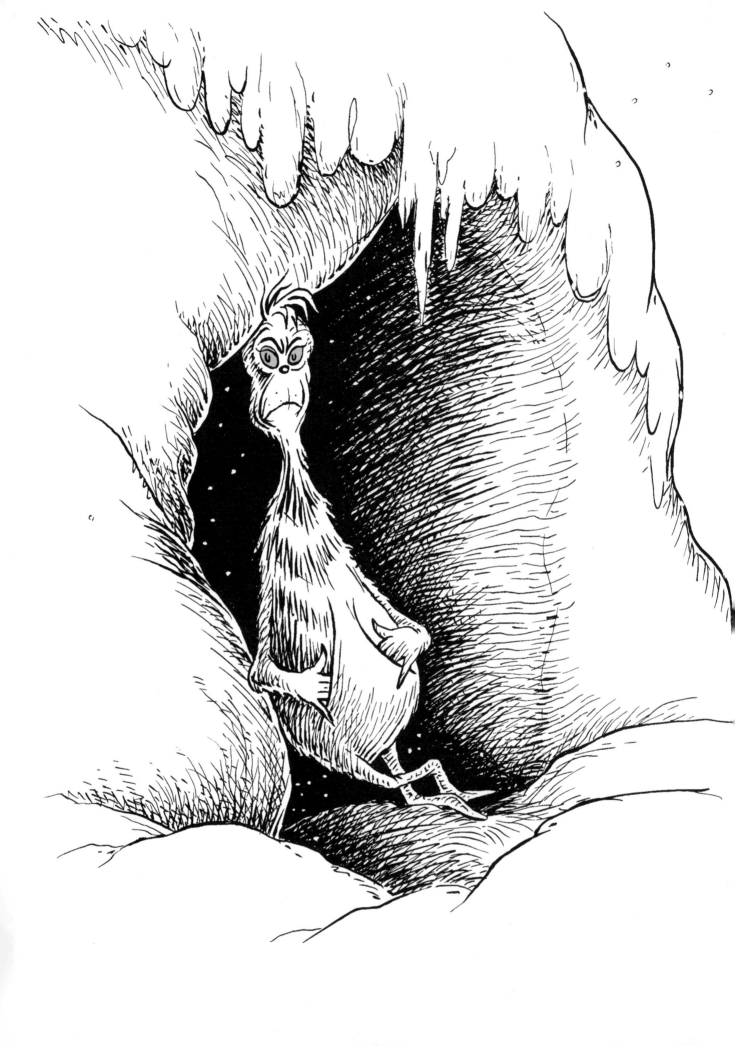

But the Grinch,
Who lived just north of *Who*-ville,
Did NOT!

The Grinch *hated* Christmas! The whole Christmas season!
Now, please don't ask why. No one quite knows the reason.
It *could* be his head wasn't screwed on just right.
It *could* be, perhaps, that his shoes were too tight.
But I think that the most likely reason of all
May have been that his heart was two sizes too small.

But,
Whatever the reason,
His heart or his shoes,
He stood there on Christmas Eve, hating the *Whos,*
Staring down from his cave with a sour, Grinchy frown
At the warm lighted windows below in their town.
For he knew every *Who* down in *Who*-ville beneath
Was busy now, hanging a mistletoe wreath.

"And they're hanging their stockings!" he snarled with a sneer.
"Tomorrow is Christmas! It's practically here!"
Then he growled, with his Grinch fingers nervously drumming,
"I MUST find some way to stop Christmas from coming!"

For,
Tomorrow, he knew . . .

MERRY MERRY

. . . All the *Who* girls and boys
Would wake bright and early. They'd rush for their toys!
And *then!* Oh, the noise! Oh, the Noise! Noise! Noise! Noise!
That's *one* thing he hated! The NOISE! NOISE! NOISE! NOISE!

Then the *Whos,* young and old, would sit down to a feast.
And they'd feast! *And they'd feast!*
And they'd FEAST!

FEAST!

FEAST!

FEAST!

They would feast on *Who*-pudding, and rare *Who*-roast-beast
Which was something the Grinch couldn't stand in the least!

And THEN
They'd do something
He liked least of all!
Every *Who* down in *Who*-ville, the tall and the small,
Would stand close together, with Christmas bells ringing.
They'd stand hand-in-hand. And the *Whos* would start singing!

They'd sing! *And they'd sing!*
AND they'd SING! SING! SING! SING!
And the more the Grinch thought of this *Who*-Christmas-Sing,
The more the Grinch thought, "I must stop this whole thing!
"Why, for fifty-three years I've put up with it now!
"I MUST stop this Christmas from coming!

>   . . . But HOW?"

Then he got an idea!
An awful idea!
THE GRINCH
GOT A WONDERFUL, AWFUL IDEA!

"I know *just* what to do!" The Grinch laughed in his throat.
And he made a quick Santy Claus hat and a coat.
And he chuckled, and clucked, "What a great Grinchy trick!
"With this coat and this hat, I look just like Saint Nick!"

"All I need is a reindeer . . ."

The Grinch looked around.

But, since reindeer are scarce, there was none to be found.

Did that stop the old Grinch . . . ?

No! The Grinch simply said,

"If I can't *find* a reindeer, I'll *make* one instead!"

So he called his dog, Max. Then he took some red thread

And he tied a big horn on the top of his head.

THEN

He loaded some bags
And some old empty sacks
On a ramshackle sleigh
And he hitched up old Max.

Then the Grinch said, "Giddap!"
And the sleigh started down
Toward the homes where the *Whos*
Lay a-snooze in their town.

All their windows were dark. Quiet snow filled the air.
All the *Whos* were all dreaming sweet dreams without care
When he came to the first little house on the square.
"This is stop number one," the old Grinchy Claus hissed
And he climbed to the roof, empty bags in his fist.

Then he slid down the chimney. A rather tight pinch.
But, if Santa could do it, then so could the Grinch.
He got stuck only once, for a moment or two.
Then he stuck his head out of the fireplace flue
Where the little *Who* stockings all hung in a row.
"These stockings," he grinned, "are the *first* things to go!"

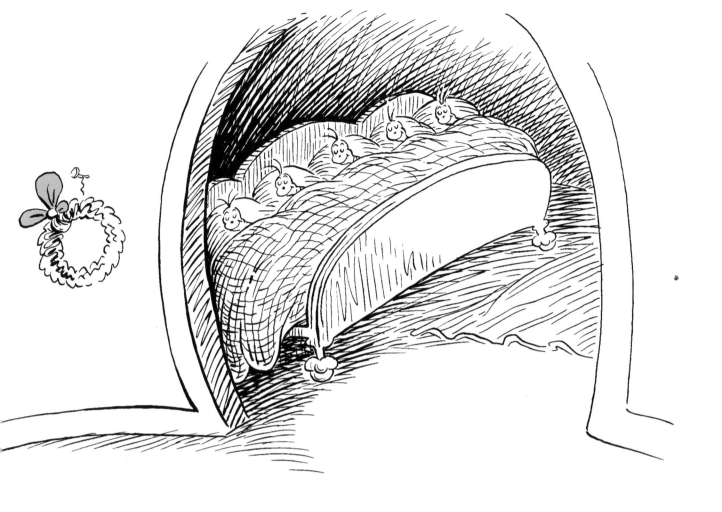

Then he slithered and slunk, with a smile most unpleasant,
Around the whole room, and he took every present!
Pop guns! And bicycles! Roller skates! Drums!
Checkerboards! Tricycles! Popcorn! And plums!
And he stuffed them in bags. Then the Grinch, very nimbly,
Stuffed all the bags, one by one, up the chimbley!

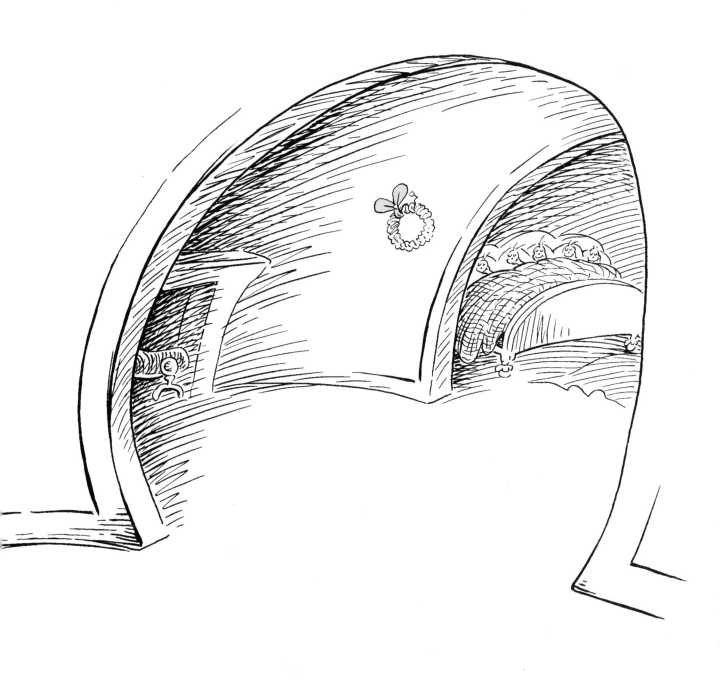

Then he slunk to the icebox. He took the *Whos'* feast!
He took the *Who*-pudding! He took the roast beast!
He cleaned out that icebox as quick as a flash.
Why, that Grinch even took their last can of *Who*-hash!

Then he stuffed all the food up the chimney with glee.
"And NOW!" grinned the Grinch, "I will stuff up the tree!"

And the Grinch grabbed the tree, and he started to shove
When he heard a small sound like the coo of a dove.
He turned around fast, and he saw a small *Who!*
Little Cindy-Lou *Who,* who was not more than two.

The Grinch had been caught by this tiny *Who* daughter
Who'd got out of bed for a cup of cold water.
She stared at the Grinch and said, "Santy Claus, why,
"*Why* are you taking our Christmas tree? WHY?"

But, you know, that old Grinch was so smart and so slick
He thought up a lie, and he thought it up quick!
"Why, my sweet little tot," the fake Santy Claus lied,
"There's a light on this tree that won't light on one side.
"So I'm taking it home to my workshop, my dear.
"I'll fix it up *there*. Then I'll bring it back *here*."

And his fib fooled the child. Then he patted her head
And he got her a drink and he sent her to bed.
And when Cindy-Lou *Who* went to bed with her cup,
HE went to the chimney and stuffed the tree up!

Then the *last* thing he took
Was the log for their fire!
Then he went up the chimney, himself, the old liar.
On their walls he left nothing but hooks and some wire.

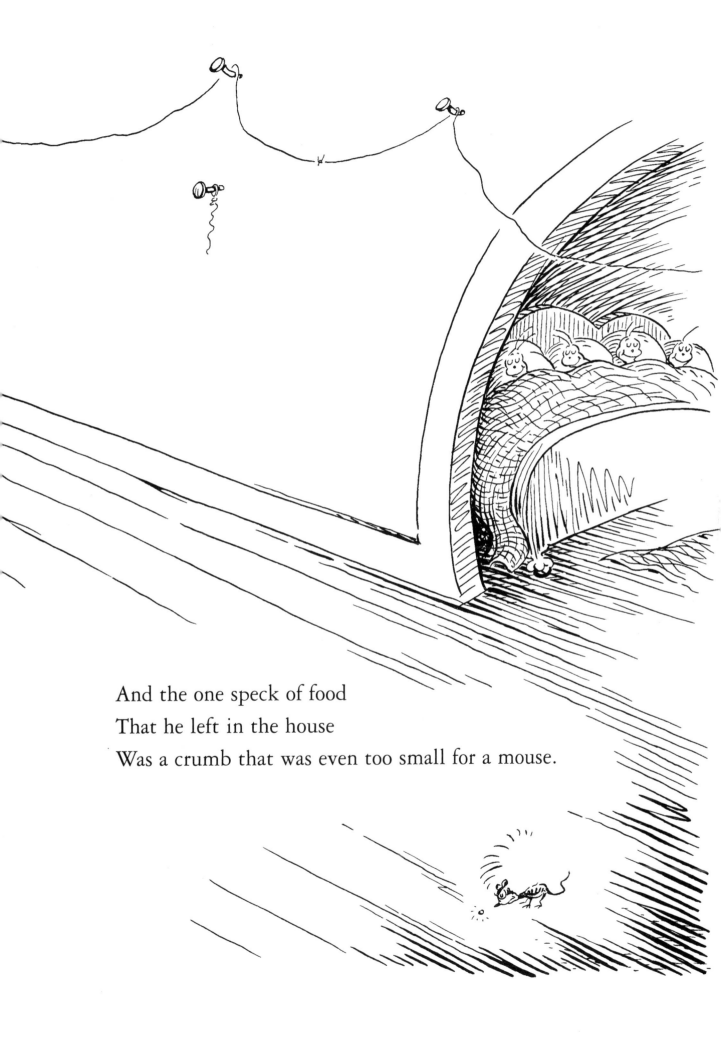

And the one speck of food
That he left in the house
Was a crumb that was even too small for a mouse.

Then
He did the *same* thing
To the *other Whos'* houses

Leaving crumbs
Much too small
For the other *Whos'* mouses!

MERRY MERRY

It was quarter past dawn . . .
    All the *Whos,* still a-bed,
    All the *Whos,* still a-snooze
When he packed up his sled,
Packed it up with their presents! The ribbons! The wrappings!
The tags! And the tinsel! The trimmings! The trappings!

Three thousand feet up! Up the side of Mt. Crumpit,
He rode with his load to the tiptop to dump it!
"Pooh-Pooh to the *Whos!*" he was grinch-ish-ly humming.
"They're finding out now that no Christmas is coming!
"They're just waking up! I know *just* what they'll do!
"Their mouths will hang open a minute or two
"Then the *Whos* down in *Who*-ville will all cry BOO-HOO!

"That's a noise," grinned the Grinch,
"That I simply MUST hear!"
So he paused. And the Grinch put his hand to his ear.
And he *did* hear a sound rising over the snow.
It started in low. Then it started to grow . . .

But the sound wasn't *sad!*
Why, this sound sounded *merry!*
It *couldn't* be so!
But it WAS merry! VERY!

He stared down at *Who*-ville!
The Grinch popped his eyes!
Then he shook!
What he saw was a shocking surprise!

Every *Who* down in *Who*-ville, the tall and the small,
Was singing! Without any presents at all!

He HADN'T stopped Christmas from coming!
IT CAME!
Somehow or other, it came just the same!

And the Grinch, with his grinch-feet ice-cold in the snow,
Stood puzzling and puzzling: "How *could* it be so?
"It came without ribbons! It came without tags!
"It came without packages, boxes or bags!"
And he puzzled three hours, till his puzzler was sore.
Then the Grinch thought of something he hadn't before!
"Maybe Christmas," he thought, *"doesn't* come from a store.
"Maybe Christmas . . . perhaps . . . means a little bit more!"

And what happened *then* . . . ?
Well . . . in *Who*-ville they say
That the Grinch's small heart
Grew three sizes that day!
And the minute his heart didn't feel quite so tight,
He whizzed with his load through the bright morning light
And he brought back the toys! And the food for the feast!
And he . . .

. . . HE HIMSELF . . . !

The Grinch carved the roast beast!

A 50TH-ANNIVERSARY

RETROSPECTIVE

by Charles D. Cohen

CHRISTMAS AND DR. SEUSS

In Iceland, he is known as Trölli. Hungarians call him Görcs. To the Japanese, he is Gurinichi. He's "der Grinch" in Germany, "il Grinch" in Italy, and "o Grinch" in Brazil. The Grinch's story is one that "subtly conveys the very essence of the meaning of Christmas while delighting and entertaining youngsters of every age. It is a story so well told that it never loses its impact, and children look forward to hearing it year after year."[1] So where did Dr. Seuss get the idea for the Grinch—a character so popular, he's become almost as much a part of Christmas as Santa and his reindeer?

He got the idea by looking in the mirror. When most people think about Dr. Seuss, they picture the Cat in the Hat, because the Cat's face shows up on the cover of so many of Dr. Seuss's Beginner Books. Dr. Seuss—whose real name was Theodor Geisel—actually *was* very playful like the Cat in the Hat. But sometimes he was also a little bit like the Grinch. In fact, Ted (as his friends and family called him) had a "GRINCH" license plate on his car for many years. "I always thought the Cat . . . was Ted on his good days, and the Grinch was Ted on his bad days,"[2] said his stepdaughter Lark Dimond-Cates.

There's no question that when Dr. Seuss created the Grinch, he was writing, in part, about himself. Dr. Seuss was fifty-three years old when he wrote *How the Grinch Stole Christmas!,* and in the book, the Grinch complains that "for fifty-three years I've put up with it now!/I MUST stop this Christmas from coming!/. . . *But HOW?*"

The worldwide appeal of the Grinch is reflected in the many versions of *How the Grinch Stole Christmas!* From left to right below: Editions from the Junior Literary Guild, Iceland, Brazil, and Germany.

Writing about the Grinch, Dr. Seuss was writing about his own concerns about the holiday. It took Ted Geisel a long time to figure out how he felt about Christmas, but, as he would later say of the Grinch, "it's not how you start out that counts. It's what you are at the finish."[3]

Growing up, Ted celebrated Christmas with his family in Springfield, Massachusetts. By the time he was twenty years old, he saw problems with some of its customs. He felt, for example, that the giving of presents wasn't appreciated the way that it should be. In his college's humor magazine, he joked that people would like a place to exchange the gifts they got for ones that they liked better, like when "brother wanted a case of Scotch and he gets a bowl of goldfish."[4]

After college, Ted kept thinking about Christmas—and not just about the presents. He also considered Santa Claus and his reindeer. When Ted was twenty-six years old, he drew a cartoon for *Judge* (a popular humor magazine in the 1920s and '30s). In it, he said that parents told their children stories featuring more characters than they could possibly remember—like Santa, his reindeer, the Stork, the Sandman, and the Boogeyman. To cut down the number of these characters, Ted decided to roll some of them together. In doing so, he created one that was part Santa Claus and part Boogeyman. He didn't call it a Grinch, but it was probably the first time Ted pictured someone other than a jolly St. Nick headed to our chimneys on Christmas Eve. In that cartoon, Ted also combined a reindeer and a stork and found that he liked the idea of strange new animals that could fly Santa to our rooftops.[5] Another time, he drew a "Santaur,"

More editions from Italy, Hungary, Japan, and France.

which looks a lot like what you'd get if you crossed Santa Claus with one of his reindeer![6]

GREEK ORIGIN: THE SANTAUR

Above: Two early experiments with Santa and reindeer. Below: Two of Ted's Christmas cards.

As he grew older, Ted kept playing with the images of Christmas, tinkering with the way that they looked but never really thinking deeply about what the holiday meant. He had a restlessly active imagination, and for him, flying reindeer weren't interesting enough to take Santa around on Christmas. As he would later write in *And to Think That I Saw It on Mulberry Street,* "Hmmmm . . . A reindeer and sleigh . . ./Say—*any*one could think of *that,*/Jack or Fred or Joe or Nat. . . ./But it isn't too late to make one little change."[7]

"Apparently, there IS a Santa Claus!"

When he was in his thirties, Ted made such changes when he created his own Christmas cards to send to friends and family. One year he drew Santa riding in a kangaroo's pouch, and in a card from another year, Santa's sleigh was pulled by five animals so strange, they made flying reindeer seem common!

After all, Reindeer are So Common!

Dr. Seuss was forty-nine years old in 1953, when he published his first Christmas story, and he was still thinking about how hard it was to find the perfect present for the holiday. In a short piece that hasn't been seen much in more than fifty years,[8] he recommended a Fluff-footed, Frizzle-topped, Three-fingered Zifft as an excellent Christmas gift (at right).

Although he would always remain sprightly and playful, Ted began to take some parts of his life more seriously around this period. During his wartime service, Ted had been concerned about the devastating effects that World War II had on a generation of children. In 1953, he and his wife, Helen, visited Japan to see first-hand the changes that had occurred. When they returned, Ted even wrote a serious article about it for *Life* magazine, although he was not happy with the edited version that was eventually published.[9] A few months later, the Korean War ended after three years of U.S. involvement. By the end of 1953, the U.S. Supreme Court was struggling with its decision about whether public schools should remain racially segregated.

In March of the next year, Ted turned fifty years old—an age at which many people begin to think about what they have done in

Perfect Present
By Dr. Seuss

If you're looking for something un-usual to send
As a present this Christmas to some good old friend,
I think you will find that an excellent gift
Is a Fluff-footed, Frizzle-topped, Three-fingered Zifft,

A fine gift to give in all gift giving seasons,
He makes a fine present for twenty-three reasons.
The first reason is: He won't talk in his sleep.
The second one is that his food is quite cheap.
The third reason is: If you go anywhere
You can take him along on the train for half fare.
The fourth reason is: He is a friendly with eagles
And won't pick a fight with your neighborhood beagles.
The fifth reason is: When you talk on the phone
He won't make a racket or blow a trombone.
The sixth reason is that this wonderful pet
Doesn't smell terribly bad when he's wet
And the rest of the reasons I sort of forget,
But I certainly *do* recommend as a gift
The Fluff-footed, Frizzle-topped, Three-fingered Zifft.

MERRY XMAS

The first Dr. Seuss Christmas piece.

their lives and what they still hope to do. Two months later, Helen was diagnosed with Guillain-Barré syndrome, a disease that paralyzed her for some time and from which she never fully recovered. Then came the Supreme Court announcement banning segregation in schools. All of these factors contributed to make this period a pivotal time in Ted's career, when the issues of mortality, accomplishment, equality, and responsibility weighed heavily on him. Also that year, an article by John Hersey in *Life* magazine criticized the books used to teach children how to read. Hersey suggested that authors like Dr. Seuss could make learning to read much more enjoyable. In August, Random House published *Horton Hears a Who!*, in which the famous elephant reflected Ted's serious interest in getting different groups to live in harmony.

In 1955, Rudolf Flesch's book *Why Johnny Can't Read and What You Can Do About It* was published. Like Hersey's article the previous year, it made Ted think about the responsibility and influence he had as a children's book writer. On December 1, 1955, Rosa Parks refused to leave her fifth-row seat on a Montgomery, Alabama, bus to make room for a white man. Martin Luther King, Jr., publicized the bus boycott that began four days later, protesting racial discrimination. Three weeks later, for Christmas 1955, *Collier's* magazine published a Dr. Seuss poem that showed a more contemplative Ted. Instead of writing about presents or what kinds of animals pulled Santa's

A PRAYER FOR A CHILD

By Dr. SEUSS

From here on earth,	Please tell all men
From my small place	That Peace is Good.
I ask of You	That's all
Way out in space:	That need be understood
Please tell all men	In every world
In every land	In Your great sky.
What You and I	(*We* understand.
Both understand . . .	Both You and I.)

sleigh, Ted wrote about the most important thing for which he could wish—a serious wish. In "A Prayer for a Child," he hoped that people around the world would learn to live together in peace. He had started thinking about the true meaning of Christmas.

The next year, in December 1956, *Redbook* magazine published a Dr. Seuss story involving a bird called the Kindly Snather.[10] Although it wasn't specifically a Christmas story, it was about learning to appreciate what you have and recognizing how your actions affect other people. The same month, *Good Housekeeping* magazine published Phyllis McGinley's story "The Year Without a Santa Claus." In it, a very tired Santa decided to take a Christmas vacation and not deliver presents. " 'Put 'em away,' roared Santa, vexed./'This year's presents will do for next./Warn the people,/Tell the papers,/I'm much too tired for Christmas capers. . . .' "[11] At first, when the children in the story heard that Santa wasn't delivering any presents, they cried so much that "their tears filled up the kitchen sinks/And cellars and empty skating rinks. . . ."[12] But one character—a six-year-old boy named Ignatius Heppelwhite—wasn't worried about not getting presents. He reminded his friends that "everyone tells me, whom I've met,/It's a day to give,/As well as to get. . . ."[13] In the story, word spread and children all over the world decided that rather than expecting gifts *from* Santa, they'd give presents *to* him. "And they had more fun, that strange December/(They said), than any they could remember."[14]

Both Dr. Seuss's story about the Kindly Snather and McGinley's story about the year without a Santa Claus made people think about someone other than themselves during the 1956 Christmas season. Ted was certainly aware of *Good Housekeeping.* Among women's magazines, it was Hearst Corporation's competitor with McCall Corporation's *Redbook,* and Ted published many stories in the latter magazine in the 1950s. In fact, four years later, *Good Housekeeping* published an article based on an interview with Dr. Seuss for its Christmas issue.[15] Therefore, while we don't know for certain that Ted read McGinley's story, it is quite likely that he did.

If so, the old question about Christmas presents must have bothered him once again. In "The Year Without a Santa Claus," not only did Santa end up delivering all his presents, but readers were reassured that Santa would continue to deliver presents every year, no matter how sick he felt or how bad the weather got. Of course, the latter part of that message echoed Robert L. May's *Rudolph the Red-Nosed Reindeer,* which preceded McGinley's story by seventeen years. Ted's concern with McGinley's story would most likely have been that despite the brief mention of Ignatius Heppelwhite's generosity and precocious wisdom, too much of "The Year Without a Santa Claus" was focused on getting presents. That message would no doubt have made Ted Geisel wonder whether presents had become more important to people than the true meaning of Christmas.

Seuss looking like a Grinch

On the day after Christmas that year, Ted looked into the mirror and got the idea for the Grinch. "I was brushing my teeth on the morning of the 26th . . . when I noted a very Grinch-ish countenance in the mirror. It was Seuss! Something had gone wrong with Christmas, I realized, or more likely with me. So I wrote the story about my sour friend, the Grinch, to see if I could rediscover something about Christmas that obviously I'd lost."[16]

Then an interesting thing happened. In 1957, three different books were published about Christmases that might not arrive! In Philadelphia, J. B. Lippincott & Co. published Phyllis McGinley's *The Year Without a Santa Claus* in book form. It was joined by Ogden Nash's *The Christmas That Almost Wasn't,* published by Little, Brown & Co. in Boston, and Dr. Seuss's *How the Grinch Stole Christmas!,* which Random House published in New York. By imagining what would happen if Christmas didn't come, these stories forced readers to consider just what Christmas really meant to them.

People liked the spirit of these new books. All three were so popular that they were made into movies. In *The Christmas That Almost Wasn't* (1966), Phineas T. Prune tried to evict the Clauses from the North Pole for not paying their rent. In the famous animated movie of Dr. Seuss's story (1966), the Grinch tried to keep Christmas from coming to Who-ville. In *The Year Without a Santa Claus* (1974), Santa, sick with the flu and depressed that no one had the Christmas spirit, decided to take the day off. But despite the popularity of the McGinley and Nash books and movies, you simply don't see many people wearing T-shirts featuring even the "good" characters like Ignatius Heppelwhite (or Thistlewhite, as he was renamed in McGinley's book), let alone the "bad" ones like Evilard or Mr. Prune. Only the Grinch, who encompasses the bad *and* the good to be found in the Christmas season, has become as important to Christmas as Rudolph and Scrooge.

How the Grinch Stole Christmas! reminds us that the holiday is about something more than presents. After all, in this story, Christmas "came without ribbons! It came without tags!/It came without packages, boxes or bags!" Dr. Seuss wanted people to realize that "maybe Christmas . . . *doesn't* come from a store./Maybe Christmas . . . means a little bit more!"

However, although that may be the easiest lesson to learn from this story, it is not necessarily the main point that Dr. Seuss was trying to make. People forget that what the Grinch liked least about Christmas wasn't the toys or the noise of children playing with them. The thing that he liked least of all was the Who-Christmas-Sing. The Grinch was an outsider who lived by himself on a mountain away from the town of Who-ville. It's kind of like being in school with a group of kids who are having fun together but don't ask you to join them. The Grinch had never felt the love that the Whos felt for their families and friends when they "would stand close together, with Christmas bells ringing. They'd stand hand-in-hand. And the *Whos* would start singing!" The Grinch had never been a part of a community. He had never felt that he belonged in any group.

How the Grinch Stole Christmas! is not just a story about whether children are going to get toys. It is a story about how the Grinch learns to enjoy the spirit of Christmas and to spend time with others so that he can become a part of their community. Unlike "The Year Without a Santa Claus," Dr. Seuss's tale doesn't end with a promise of presents every year. It ends when the Grinch sits down to dinner with the Whos and joins them in warm fellowship. It's the same message that Seuss put into "A Prayer for a Child." Dr. Seuss wanted to teach children that even though people may look different or come from different places, they can come together as friends. And even though this is a Christmas tale, Dr. Seuss never mentions religion in the story. In fact, he claimed, "I spent three months on the last page of 'The Grinch.' It kept turning into a religious tract."[17] The real message of the book is about finding the true spirit of friendship and community.

The book became one of Dr. Seuss's most popular. Earlier in the same year that Random House published *How the Grinch Stole Christmas!,* it also published *The Cat in the Hat.* The two books made Dr. Seuss so famous that by the end of the year, he had received 9,267 *pounds* of fan mail![18] He was soon getting thousands of letters each week.

Dr. Seuss said that *How the Grinch Stole Christmas!* was written "in one month, and illustrated in two months," but that "in spite of the rush and pressure . . . [it] turned out to be one of my best books."[19] The reason it was so successful is that Ted seamlessly blended his longtime interest in playfully altering the images of Christmas with his more serious desire to remind people of the message and spirit of the holiday. In doing so, he chose to share with the world an unflattering part of himself—the Grinchy part that got cranky about holiday hoopla, tidings, and trappings. Most readers can recognize some of the Grinch's feelings in themselves, which is why, half a century later, nearly everyone—everywhere—knows the Grinch.

THE GRINCH

1957: What color is the Grinch? We all think of him as being green. But the Grinch has changed a lot over the last fifty years. He's gotten a new look in almost every decade. When Dr. Seuss's book first appeared in October 1957, the Grinch was black and white with pink eyes. He didn't turn green until 1966, when animator Chuck Jones made his famous cartoon version of the book.[1] In 1977, Dr. Seuss wrote a story for television called *Halloween Is Grinch Night,* and Gerard Baldwin gave the Grinch a different look for that cartoon. Dr. Seuss wrote a script in 1982 in which two of his most famous characters meet, called *The Grinch Grinches the Cat in the Hat.* Bill Perez gave the Grinch a new appearance in that show, and Dr. Seuss revealed more to us about the Grinch's background, introducing viewers to the Grinch's mother. In Ron Howard's 2000 feature-film version of the book, the Grinch got another makeover, and even more of the Grinch's "backstory" was suggested (obviously *not* by Dr. Seuss). The advertising for that movie gave the Grinch yet another new image, this time as "da Grinch," to try to appeal to the extreme-sports and hip-hop demographics. But despite all of these changes, there's something special about the original Grinch that continues to endear him to each new generation without gimmickry.

In fact, Dr. Seuss's character has remained so popular that he has changed the meaning of the word "grinch"! As far back as anyone can remember, "grinched" meant that something was closed very tightly. If you were really cold, your teeth might be grinched together. Your hands could be grinched into fists if you were mad, and your eyes could be grinched shut if you were scared.[2] Later, the word "grinch" was used to describe making a harsh grating sound.[3] Eventually, Dr. Seuss's version of the word "grinch" was officially added to dictionaries, defined as "a spoilsport or killjoy"[4] or "a person or thing that spoils or dampens the pleasure of others."[5] Even the FBI used the new meaning when it posted a Fraud Alert on the Internet for Christmas 2003, with the warning headline "Don't be

'Grinched' this holiday season."[6] The Grinch actually changed the English language!

So how did Dr. Seuss's Grinch get his look? When Ted Geisel first created a character called a Grinch in 1953, it wasn't the one that we know now—it was a bird! In *Scrambled Eggs Super!* one of the birds that Peter T. Hooper passed (because it wasn't laying eggs that day) was the Beagle-Beaked-Bald-Headed Grinch.

Ted's next Grinch—which appeared two years later in the short story "The Hoobub and the Grinch"—didn't look much like the famous character either. In that story, Grinches were creatures who convinced others to buy things that they didn't need.[7] A Hoobub learned that lesson while relaxing outdoors, after his sunbathing was interrupted by a Grinch trying to sell him a piece of green string.

Ironically, at the same time that Ted presented a Grinch convincing other creatures to buy things they didn't need, he used an early version of the classic Grinch in an advertisement enticing people to buy Holly Sugar! In a further ironic twist, the sugar company used some of Ted's advertisements on billboards, but he was fired after he created a pamphlet for his local town council to help try to ban billboards!

The Grinch in the Holly Sugar ad was very similar to the famous Grinch that appeared in the Dr. Seuss book,

Right and below: Two early "Grinches."

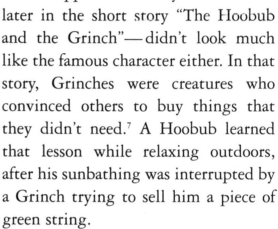

The Hoobub and the Grinch

BY DR. SEUSS

The Hoobub was lying outdoors in the sun,
The wonderful, wonderful, warm summer sun.
"There's *nothing*," he said, "quite as good as the sun!"

Then, up walked a Grinch with a piece of green string.
"How much," asked the Grinch, "will you pay for this thing?
You sure ought to have it. You'll find it great fun.
And it's worth a lot more than that old-fashioned sun."
"Huh . . . ?" asked the Hoobub. "Sounds silly to me.
Worth more than the sun . . . ? Why, that surely can't be."
"But it *is!*" grinned the Grinch. "Let me give you the reasons.

The sun's only good in a couple short seasons.
For you'll have to admit that in winter and fall
The sun is quite weak. It is not strong at all.
*But this wonderful piece of green string I have here
Is strong, my good friend, every month of the year!*"
"Even so . . ." said the Hoobub, "I still sort of doubt . . ."
"But you *know*," yapped the Grinch, and he started to shout,
"That *sometimes* the sun doesn't even come out!
But this marvelous piece of green string, I declare,
*Can come out of your pocket, if you keep it there,
Any time, day or night! Any place! Anywhere!*"

"Hmm . . ." said the Hoobub. "That *would* be quite handy . . ."
"This piece of green string," yelled the Grinch, "is a dandy!
That sun, let me tell you, is dangerous stuff!
It can freckle your face. It can make your skin rough.
When the sun gets too hot, it can broil you like fat!
But this piece of green string, sir, will NEVER do that!
THIS PIECE OF GREEN STRING IS COLOSSAL! IMMENSE!
AND, TO YOU . . . WELL, I'LL SELL IT FOR 98 CENTS!"
And the Hoobub . . . *he bought!*
(And I'm sorry to say
That Grinches sell Hoobubs such things every day.)

published two years later. He had the same sourpuss face and pointy fingers.[8] Ted suggested that "the Grinch looks a little like Bennett Cerf" (his publisher at Random House).[9] The Grinch maintained that basic look from 1957 to 1966.

Of course, the Holly Sugar Grinch was green. . . .

1966: The Grinch's look began to change when Dr. Seuss and Chuck Jones created their television special from the book. The Grinch took on the colors of Christmas, with green fur underneath a red Santa suit. This new version of the Grinch bore an interesting (but probably coincidental) resemblance to a character from Dr. Seuss's and Jones's childhoods called the Tempter[10]—a scary creature used in advertisements about the danger of fire.

Chuck Jones knew Ted Geisel from their work together on army films during World War II. Back then, Ted wasn't making much money from his children's books, and Jones remembered him saying that "if he could only earn $5,000 or $6,000 a year from his books' royalties then he'd never have to worry about finances."[11] Years later, the animator called to ask about pro-

ducing one of Ted's children's books for television. As Jones recalled, "I figured maybe he could use some extra money."[12]

Jones wasn't aware that Ted's children's books had made him a

Ted Geisel and Chuck Jones at work on the animated version of *How the Grinch Stole Christmas!*

multimillionaire. He didn't need the paycheck. But he had other reasons to want to work with Jones. Ted had been offered lots of money to let others use his characters in television shows, but nobody wanted him to be involved in the productions. Ted turned everyone down because, as he put it, they wanted him to "kindly stay home and let us tend to the TV business. With Chuck, I knew I could work actively with him on the Grinch."[13] Ted also did not like the cost-cutting measures that TV producers used. He felt that their short-sighted approach led to characters that, as interviewer Hal Humphrey described, "jump and jerk around like puppets on strings, instead of flowing smoothly. . . ."[14] According to one source, while most cartoons of that era used about two thousand drawings for a show of that length, *"The Grinch* required about twenty-five thousand."[15]

Ted's instincts were appreciated and rewarded. In 1970, a Peabody Award was given to "The Dr. Seuss Programs," apparently intended for both *How the Grinch Stole Christmas!* and *Horton Hears a Who!* Specific mention was made of the "superb example of how an inspired children's book can be translated into an equally entrancing television show—IF the author is allowed to work on the script himself and pick the right people to help him with the job. In this case, Dr. Seuss . . . enlisted the services of an old side-kick . . . Chuck Jones," as co-producer, and their effort made "crystal clear why Dr. Seuss is, by all odds, the most popular author of . . . [children's books] in America."

When production began on the cartoon in September 1965,[16] half of CBS's programming was still done in black and white.[17]

We take it for granted that what we see on television is in color, but in the 1950s, when Ted wrote his book, only special events were broadcast in color, like presidential addresses, the World Series, or star-studded musical specials. In addition, not many people had televisions that could display those programs in color. By the early 1960s, as more people began to own color television sets, a greater

number of programs were shown in color.[18] But even in late 1963, an event as important as the assassination of President Kennedy was seen on the news across America in black and white. Making the Grinch green was an important change—one that accommodated the increased use of color on TV.

For the Christmas season of 1965, CBS had debuted Charles Schulz's first animated television special, *A Charlie Brown Christmas*.[19] For Christmas 1966, the network planned to air *How the Grinch Stole Christmas!* CBS's fall schedule that year was the first with all of its prime-time shows in color. Outside of that popular time block, the day's schedule wouldn't be filled with color shows until 1967—the year that the first color broadcasts in Europe took place.[20] It was against this backdrop that the green Grinch was unveiled on December 18, 1966.

Dr. Seuss's biggest additions to the television cartoon were the words to the songs. "Trim Up the Tree" names many of the colorful toys and decorations from the Whos' Christmas celebration, like Bingel Balls, Goo Hoogungs, Bizzel Binks, Wungs, Hoo Boo Boobicks, Pan Tookas, Pam Poonas, Fuzzel Fuzz, Bliffer Bloofs, Wuzzel Wuzz, Dafflers, Snaffer Snoof, and Dang-Donglers. However, the most memorable lyrics were the descriptions of the Grinch in "You're a Mean One, Mr. Grinch." The book's simple black-and-white Grinch with pink eyes grew into a Grinch with garlic in his soul, termites in his smile, and a heart full of unwashed socks—a heart alternatively described as "a dead tomato

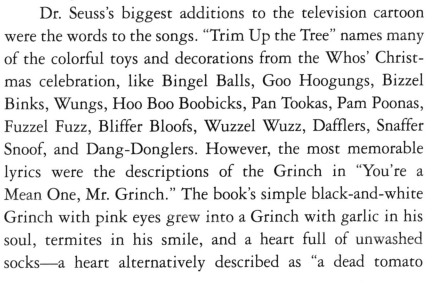

The Grinch in repose, as Ted originally conceived him in his 1957 book (top left), and his transformation under Chuck Jones in 1966.

splotched with moldy purple spots!" This was, after all, a character who would abuse his pet dog, break into and burglarize homes, and lie to a child's face.

1977: There are two other animated Grinch television specials that are less well known than Chuck Jones's version. *Halloween Is Grinch Night* debuted on ABC on October 28, 1977, and went on to win an Emmy Award for Outstanding Children's Special—Primetime. Dr. Seuss's acceptance speech was noted for its delightful brevity:

The Grinch gets a new look for *Halloween Is Grinch Night* (1977).

> In our studio out in Van Nuys,
> There are so many great gals and great guys.
> If I thanked them all,
> We'd be here until fall,
> And I don't think that would be wise.[21]

Gerard Baldwin directed the cartoon, for which Dr. Seuss kept some of the familiar characters and added a few new ones. The Grinch, Max, and the Whos were joined by animals like Gree-grumps, Hakken-krakks (spelled slightly differently in *Oh, the Places You'll Go!*), and a Wuzzy Woozo.

It was the singing of the Whos that irked the Grinch in *How the Grinch Stole Christmas!* and made him head into Who-ville. This time, it was the howling of the Hakken-krakks in Who-ville's Punker's Pond that irritated the Grinch and drove him out of his cave to take his anger out on the Whos.

This Grinch had a paunchier stomach but maintained the same dark collar of fur that Chuck Jones dreamed up. He looked a bit frazzled, and his eyebrows seemed to have a life of their own—they left his face and flew around like a bird under his command during one song. This Grinch seemed just as mean-spirited—he'd double back to run over a flower that he missed crushing. But like most Halloween spooks, this frightening Grinch was full of bluster and trickery rather than genuine menace. Even his voice, supplied by

Hans Conried instead of Boris Karloff, sounded more irritated and comical than scary.

1982: At the end of *Halloween Is Grinch Night,* the Grinch warned, "I'll be coming back someday." And he did return to television five years later in *The Grinch Grinches the Cat in the Hat.* Bill Perez directed the cartoon, which was first broadcast on May 20, 1982, and won two Emmy Awards (for Outstanding Animated Program and for Outstanding Individual Achievement in Animated Programming).

It is in this movie that we learned the Grinch's Oath:

A Grinch is unhelpful, unfriendly, unkind,
with ungracious thoughts in an unhealthy mind.
A Grinch is uncheerful, uncouth, and unclean.
Now say this together: "We're frightfully mean!"[22]

The dark collar, extra paunch, and prominent eyebrows defined the Grinch in *Halloween Is Grinch Night* (top). For *The Grinch Grinches the Cat in the Hat* (bottom), the Grinch was given a darker shade of green and less neck fur.

This Grinch looked more like Ted's original one, but kept the green color that had become so strongly associated with him. His voice was more like that in the original cartoon version and, unlike the Grinch in *Grinch Night,* this one was more than just bluster. He created machines to control what others could hear and see.

The Grinch Grinches the Cat in the Hat displayed the two sides of Ted Geisel. Way back in 1920, he had written some jokes for his high school paper—some as Ole the Optimist and others as Pete the Pessimist. More than sixty years later, those two aspects of Ted's personality met again in this cartoon

and did battle. When the pessimistic and mean Grinch couldn't drive past the optimistic and cheerful Cat's car, the Cat apologized for "blockerizing and obstructivating" the roadway. But after the Cat in the Hat referred to the Grinch as "Mr. Greenface," the Grinch suffered from road rage and hounded the Cat. He used an Acoustical Anti-Audial Bleeper (also known as a Vacu-Sound-Sweeper) to control sound and keep the Cat from talking, while the Grinch sang:

I am the boss
of what everyone hears.
The sound of your voice
is the sound of my choice.
I am the master
of everyone's ears.[23]

Despite their conflict, the optimistic Cat wanted to find out what made the Grinch so sour and mean. In the song "Why Is a Grinch?" the Cat pondered how he could establish communication with the Grinch:

Deep inside his freaky freakness,
there must be a soft spot.
There must be a weakness.
Despite the grim fact
that he's depraved and deranged,
I will find that soft spot.
That Grinch can be changed![24]

In the Cat's efforts to understand the Grinch, we learned about the Grinch's background for the first time, discovering that he did care about someone after all—his mother.

The Grinch survived these many different looks and stories to remain one of the most recognizable characters in all of children's literature. Fifty years after Random House first published *How the Grinch Stole*

Christmas!, the book and its characters are so popular that they have become part of the public consciousness. If "imitation is the sincerest form of flattery," Dr. Seuss gets complimented all the time. The innumerable references people make to his book provide clear evidence that it has become an integral part of popular culture.

TV has been a fertile ground for these references. The Grinch himself appeared in an episode of the animated program *Family Guy,* in a rooftop battle with Peter Griffin's neighbor, policeman Joe Swanson.[25] A character called the Grinch appeared with henchmen on *Johnny Bravo,*[26] *Hang Time* had a Grinch Santa,[27] *South Park* had the Grinchiepoo,[28] and *Tiny Toon Adventures* had a Blue Grinch who referred to "all the shmagoos down in Shmagooville."[29] Several shows have also used the image of the Grinch's heart growing three sizes (for example, *South Park,*[30] *My Life as a Teenage Robot,*[31] and *The Venture Brothers*[32]).

Actress Gina Gershon starred in an episode of *Snoops* titled "The Grinch,"[33] and Kelsey Grammer was the title character in the episode of *Frasier* entitled "Frasier Grinch."[34] Allusions to the title of the book have been made in television episodes like "How the Ghosts Stole Christmas" (*The X-Files*),[35] "How the Finch Stole Christmas" (*Just Shoot Me!*[36] and *ER*[37]), "The Finster Who Stole Christmas" (*All Grown Up*),[38] "The Cheese Who Stole Christmas" (*Samurai Pizza Cats*),[39] "The Wood Who Stole Christmas" (*Evening Shade,* with Burt Reynolds playing Wood Newton),[40] "How the Super Stoled Christmas" (*The PJs,* with Eddie Murphy voicing the superintendent),[41] "The Crybaby Who Stole Christmas" (*Nikki*),[42] "The Mom That Stole Christmas" (*The Geena Davis Show*),[43] and "The Big How the Ex Stole Christmas Episode" (*Half & Half*).[44] While discussing cool holiday shows on *Beavis and Butt-head,* Butt-head came up with "The Grunge Who Stole Christmas."[45]

The Whos were evoked by the singing people encircling the town square in a 1990 episode of *The Simpsons.*[46] In a 2005 episode of *House,* cancer patient Cindy Kramer's innocence led the titular doctor to insist, "I still don't treat Cindy-Lou Who."[47]

Other allusions have appeared on *The Pretender,*[48] *King of the*

The first information about the Grinch's background was divulged in *The Grinch Grinches the Cat in the Hat,* in which the Grinch's mother appears.

Hill,[49] *That '70s Show,*[50] *Buffy the Vampire Slayer,*[51] *Made in Canada,*[52] *Buzz Lightyear of Star Command,*[53] *Lizzie McGuire,*[54] *Committed,*[55] *South Park,*[56] and in other episodes of *The Simpsons.*[57, 58, 59]

Of course, these references are not limited to television. A dispute between opposing lawyers in Dallas about working through the holiday season prompted one of them to write "How the Grinch Stole Christmas Vacation,"[60] which circulated widely on the Internet. Also passed around on the Web were parodies supporting both sides in the 2000 U.S. presidential election, like "How the Grinch Stole the Election" and "How Al Sore Stole the Election by Dr. Ruse,"[61] as well as a response to the September 11, 2001, terrorist attacks called "The Binch"[62] and the insightful (or inciteful?) 2005 satire "How the Liberals Stole Christmas (or) A Visit from St. Dick."[63] Random House itself has published political works with similar titles, like *How the Republicans Stole Christmas: The Republican Party's Declared Monopoly on Religion and What Democrats Can Do to Take It Back*[64] and *The Judge Who Stole Christmas.*[65]

The story line and characters of *How the Grinch Stole Christmas!* have struck a chord with so many people that they have simply become ingrained in the public psyche. They can easily be mentioned in virtually any context with assurance that the listener shares the frame of reference.

MAX

One of the first times Dr. Seuss experimented with alternatives to traditional reindeer was during college in 1922, when one of his teachers took him and his friend Frederick "Pete" Blodgett to a cabin in the mountains to go hunting. Pete brought along his pet beagle, Spot, and Ted drew a picture of Spot with antlers.[1]

The idea of a dog with antlers stuck with him, and over time, Ted found other dogs that he thought looked even funnier with horns than a beagle. Five years later, for Christmas 1927, Ted invented the Dachs-Deer for a magazine where he worked, commenting, "It is no everyday feat . . . to cross a reindeer with a dachshund!"[2] He liked that idea and drew another dachshund-reindeer seven years later for a different magazine. Ted

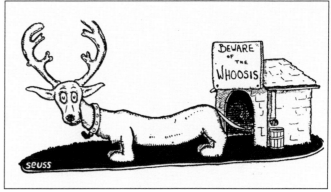

eventually began spelling "Dachs-Deer" as "Dax-Deer," which was probably unconsciously based on the Grinch's artificially antlered dog, Max, whom we might call the Max-Deer.

The endearing quality of Ted's artwork becomes apparent when his renditions of odd characters are compared with similar beasts created by others. The Steven Manufacturing Company produced several

Clockwise from top right: Max as deer (1957), 1927 Dachs-Deer, 1934 crossbreed, and 1960s Dax-Deer.

Dr. Seuss

A DAX-Deer

1,647,829 B.C. Experiments between reindeer and dachshund result in fiasco.

73

ceramic figures in 1972 that depicted animals of mixed breeding, including a "Dachsheer." In contrast to Ted's animal, this more literal representation appears more freakish than friendly.

Dr. Seuss described the Grinch's faithful dog, Max, as "Everydog—all love and limpness and loyalty,"[3] which is exactly why so many people have fallen in love

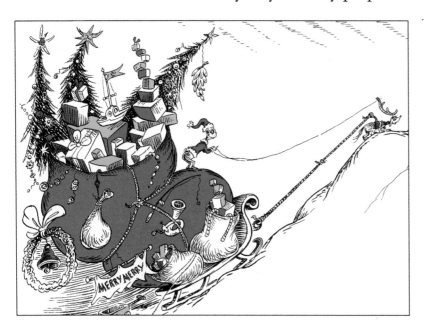

with Max in the book and, even more so, in the 1966 cartoon version. For many people, Chuck Jones's animated dog was particularly memorable, as Jones gave the beleaguered sidekick—whose name is only mentioned twice in the entire book—a lot more personality and visibility.

Max gets to express himself even more in the

The charm of Dr. Seuss's characters is evident when comparing Steven Manufacturing Company's vision of a crossbred dog-deer (Dachsheer, top right) to Max—whether he's pulling the Grinch's sleigh up Mt. Crumpit in the book (middle left) or his Paraphernalia Wagon in *Halloween Is Grinch Night* (bottom).

1977 cartoon *Halloween Is Grinch Night.* Just as he had to pull the overloaded sleigh full of toys up Mt. Crumpit in *How the Grinch Stole Christmas!,* Max has to haul the Grinch's massive Paraphernalia Wagon in *Halloween Is Grinch Night.* While he wearily pulls the wagon (which holds nightmares that the Grinch can release on the Whos), Max sings a song about how ashamed of him his aunt Woofie Woofoon must be. He asks himself,

> Why am I the slave of
> This Grinchy old grock?
> And I say,
> "How I wish
> I could turn back the clock
> And have the fine future
> I once had before
> And again be an innocent puppy once more. . . ."[4]

The unhappy Max dutifully does what his tyrannical master demands in all three films. However, as the Grinch's weaknesses come to light, there are glimpses of Max's increasing confidence in the films. By the end of *Halloween Is Grinch Night,* Max stands up to the Grinch by giving him a loud "raspberry" and running away. Finally, in *The Grinch Grinches the Cat in the Hat,* Max gets the last laugh, turning the sound-altering Acoustical Anti-Audial Bleeper on the Grinch to shut him up for good.

Max hung helplessly at the Grinch's whim in the cartoons *How the Grinch Stole Christmas!* (left) and *The Grinch Grinches the Cat in the Hat* (center). But Max got the last laugh in the latter film (right).

THE WHOS

Three years before the world was introduced to the Grinch, we met the Whos when Horton saved them from destruction in Dr. Seuss's book *Horton Hears a Who!* The idea for a place inhabited by small people no doubt had stayed with Ted Geisel from his youth, when he admired Palmer Cox's Brownies, was exposed to William Donahey's Teenie Weenies, and enjoyed Jonathan Swift's Lilliputians in *Gulliver's Travels.*

Ted said, "I loved the Brownies—they were wonderful little creatures; in fact, they probably awakened my desire to draw."[1] He also said that he "was very interested in Jonathan Swift"[2] and had a particular fondness for *Gulliver's Travels.*[3] His interest in Swift was so great that he claimed he went from Oxford's Lincoln College to the Sorbonne specifically to study Swift with Emile Legouis.[4] At age seventy-five, when Ted created a list of sixty-five people who had inspired, helped, or encouraged him, Swift was the fourth name on the list.[5]

Ted's Whos (top) were inspired by other small creatures he read about as a child, like Palmer Cox's Brownies (bottom).

In fact, without his even realizing it, Ted's amazing memory seems to have stored a lot of information about Gulliver's Lilliputians. In Swift's book, the Lilliputians were at war with the people of Blefuscu over whether the large or small end of an egg should be broken in order to eat it. That is exactly the sort of senseless culinary conflict that we find in Dr. Seuss's *The Butter Battle Book,* in which the Yooks, who eat their bread butter-side up, go to war with the Zooks because they eat their bread butter-side down.

Just as the Big-endians and Small-endians appear to be the model for the Butter-Down Zooks and Butter-Up Yooks, the tiny Lilliputians seem to be the basis for the Whos. In *Horton Hears a Who!,* the emphasis is on the size difference between Horton and the Whos, which enables Horton to protect them. Similarly, in *Gulliver's Travels,* the key feature is the size difference between Lemuel Gulliver and the Lilliputians, which, for example, allows Gulliver to save their emperor's palace from fire.

But when Ted Geisel was working on *Horton Hears a Who!,* his wife, Helen, looked at the Whos he had drawn and told him that they looked like bugs. That wasn't too surprising. When Dr. Seuss first started making a name for himself, it wasn't because of his children's books. He initially became famous for the bugs that he drew in his advertisements for Flit bug spray. His insects were so popular that he used them in other ads, like the one he did for Dupont Cellophane. Some of those bugs *do* look a lot like Whos.

Helen convinced him to alter the look of the Whos. She told him, "They are not bugs. . . . Those Whos are . . . small people."[6] Ted changed them into the Whos who have charmed us in two books, the cartoons based on those books, and *Halloween Is Grinch Night.* But a key to their charm lies in the slightly insectoid features that Ted instinctively knew were necessary to make a Who.

Ted developed the Whos from the insects he drew in advertisements and cartoons. Compare Ted's Whos (bottom left, top left, and top second from right) to his earlier work for Dupont Cellophane (middle left), Flit bug spray (top second from left), and *Life* magazine (top right).

Watching children care for their small plush toys and dolls, one can see how they like to protect small creatures. This is one reason that the Whos are so endearing to children. The small Whos always seem to need someone bigger to look out for them. In *Horton Hears a Who!,* the big kangaroo enlists the help of the Wickersham Brothers

to try to take the dust speck on which the Whos live and boil it "in a hot steaming kettle of Beezle-Nut oil." In *How the Grinch Stole Christmas!*, the Grinch steals all of their toys and tries to ruin their celebration. And in *Halloween Is Grinch Night,* the Grinch heads into Who-ville to threaten them once again.

But the Whos aren't just cute. When they're celebrating and having fun, they can be noisy, and their noisemaking shows us another step in their development. In the 1930s, in addition to the bugs that Ted drew for Flit ads, he also created raucous creatures called Wild Tones for an advertising booklet to promote Stromberg-Carlson radios.

In a fascinating example of his visual memory, Ted combined two Wild Tones from the same page in that booklet into the image of one Who in the book *How the Grinch Stole Christmas!,* without even realizing it. In the booklet, one spiky-haired Wild Tone is suspended horizontally in midair. With a round mitt on the end of his thin arm, a second Wild Tone bangs a bass drum adorned with a series of *Y*-shapes. In the book, Ted fused these two images into one spiky-haired Who suspended in a horizontal position, beating a bass drum decorated with the same *Y*-shapes, and holding a thin-handled drumstick topped by a round striking end. It's hard to believe that these images, right down to the cloud puffs representing the drums' noise, were separated by at least two decades.

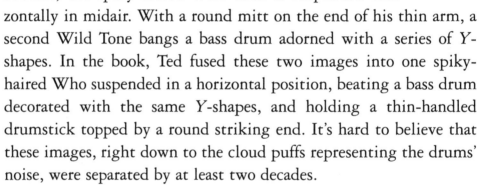

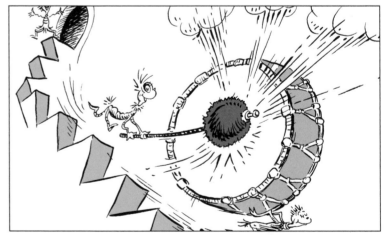

Ted made ties between the Whos in *Horton Hears a Who!* and *How the Grinch Stole Christmas!* In the earlier book, Who-ville is ultimately saved by Jo-Jo, who issues the final "YOPP!" In the later one, as the Grinch first reaches out from the chimney he has descended, the presents in the room include a tricycle intended "for Jo-Jo."[7]

For Jones, the Whos were so interchangeable that he even used the same cel in his productions of both *How the Grinch Stole Christmas!* and *Horton Hears a Who!* We first see the image when the Grinch worries that on Christmas morning, the Whos will "blow their Floo Floobers, they'll bang their Tah Tinkers." The same image turns up in the later cartoon when Doc Hoovey urges the Whos to "play on a pizzer" (or anything else) to make noise so that they can be heard by the animals trying to destroy their dust speck.

Chuck Jones tried to work faithfully from Dr. Seuss's originals. Jones mentioned that in studying the Whos, he realized that, for example, Cindy-Lou Who "is not a regular little girl—she has antennas,"[8] much like the bugs that Helen Geisel had worried about. In the process of stylizing the Whos, Jones transformed the insect-like Cindy-Lou Who into a memorable, doe-eyed young girl—with antennas.

Jones kept Who features like Cindy-Lou's antennas (center left), but greatly stylized them (center right).

If you like the Whos, you can meet another Who family in *Halloween Is Grinch Night.* Ukariah Who is the nearsighted young boy who bravely faces the Grinch to protect his grandfather Josiah, grandmother Mariah, sister Bethiah, and brother Obediah.

Apparently, though, many people who are fond of the Whos in the books and earlier movies do not find the Whos in *Halloween Is Grinch Night* as appealing. Lacking any hint of insect ancestry, the blinking Ukariah looks a bit too human to be a Who, while his grandfather Josiah looks more like a flower than a bug or a small man. In part, this

The very differently styled Whos in *Halloween Is Grinch Night* are represented by Ukariah (bottom).

may explain why *Halloween Is Grinch Night* never gained the same popularity with audiences as *How the Grinch Stole Christmas!*

The Whos, the Grinch, and Max have all undergone changes over the years. If Ted had not been so committed to experimenting and making improvements, we'd all be singing:

> Who noo neebu!
> Who doo deebu!
> Welcome, Christmas! Christmas cheer!
> Nuh who norbick!
> Duh who dorbick!
> Cheer to all so near and dear.
> Welcome, Christmas!
> Who fla floobik!
> Welcome, Christmas!
> Who na noobik![9]

With that in mind, it is important to note that Ted kept tight control over his creations, so he was directly involved with many of the changes made to the Grinch, Max, and the Whos over the years. He obviously didn't feel that his characters had to be completely static and immutable entities. Some of the innovations, like the greenness of the Grinch, were so successful that they have almost replaced Ted's original vision. Therefore, it would be wrong to suggest that no one should ever pursue new versions of his characters. However, some of the other modifications of Ted's characters (including many of the changes made in movies and books since his death in 1991) have been much less successful and have met with strong disapproval from Dr. Seuss fans. The key seems to be finding a way to create something new and intriguing without losing the elements that make the original Dr. Seuss characters unforgettable and beloved. These characters are not in danger of becoming stagnant. There are, after all, good reasons that *How the Grinch Stole Christmas!* has remained vibrant, meaningful, and memorable for half a century thus far.

What would Ted have made of this fiftieth-anniversary edition of his book? Initially, I suspect he'd have been wary of the analysis. When asked what he thought about PhD theses based on his work, Ted replied, "I think they're a ridiculous waste of time. . . . People who are working for their doctorates . . . [will] take a book of mine that has one color in it and talk about my great sensitivity in handling that color, and why I chose that color, when the fact is that Bennett Cerf [Ted's publisher at Random House] called me up one morning and said, 'We're having a bit of a financial problem, so cut down your colors.'"[10] In part, Ted was too modest to think of his children's books as worthy of scholarly study. Based on his own experiences as a student, he also had some questions about the picayune details of postgraduate work. Most importantly, as he told one interviewer who asked him if he had plans to write his memoirs, Ted believed "it's the product that's most important, not the process of how it was created."[11]

On the other hand, Ted's desire to tell good stories was often stronger than his need to tell the truth. He was prone to exaggeration and fabrication in the name of a laugh or a clever idea. So his work begs for someone to take the time to uncover the firsthand sources and stick closely to them to determine the facts about his creations. His family, friends, and co-workers have generally been very pleased with this kind of fact-based analysis.

The reality is that Ted would probably have been surprised to see how each of his characters developed, because he didn't seem to recognize how tenaciously his memory held on to various images and how he returned, unconsciously, to revisit some themes throughout his life. When asked how much his early childhood influenced his work, Ted answered, "Not to a very great extent. . . . Generally speaking, I don't think my childhood influenced my work. I think I skipped my childhood."[12] Yet in other interviews, he would tell an anecdote from his youth and explain that the incident was the basis for a certain story or book. And there are images Ted saw as a child—in books and around his hometown—that show up repeatedly in his work.

These conflicting statements illustrate the value of finding and presenting the truth about how a book like *How the Grinch Stole*

Ted poses
in front of
storyboards
for the 1966
production of
*How the Grinch
Stole Christmas!*

Christmas! developed, because even Ted was unaware of some of his sources. Another benefit is that in the process, certain items have been uncovered that the public has been unable to see for five decades or more. Although some of these rarities might embarrass Ted today (since he was a perfectionist and would certainly regard his early efforts with apprehension), it is critical to keep these treasures from being lost, and Seuss fans are likely to be excited to have the opportunity to enjoy them.

Despite the healthy view he kept of his work, Ted did feel that "writing children's books is a sweat-and-blood thing. You have to get in there and cut and prune and throw your best passages out, because a writer's best passages . . . are usually beyond the ken of children. . . ."[13] Often he agonized for a year at a time on his books. It was stressful work to make his verse flow so easily, which is why attempts to mimic his rhythm and rhyme are routinely awful. But there was something special about Christmas that had obviously been building inside of Ted for many years before he wrote *How the Grinch Stole Christmas!* because it took him just three months[14] to produce one of the best-known holiday stories of all time, popularly judged to be a classic piece of American fiction. Hopefully, Ted would have been proud that a sincere and loving effort was made to frame one of his masterworks and provide a factual perspective on it.

ENDNOTES

In an attempt to standardize the vast field of Seussiana, Charles Cohen has cataloged his extensive collection and given each piece a unique identifier. Some endnotes include these reference codes, which appear in brackets and are placed within or at the end of the note, where applicable.

CHRISTMAS AND DR. SEUSS

1. Janet Serlin Garber, "Teacher's Discussion Guide" from the *How the Grinch Stole Christmas!* filmstrip set (Westminster, MD: Random House Educational Media, 1976), 4 [CC197612z0105].
2. Lark Dimond-Cates, speech at the United States Postal Service's unveiling of the Theodor Seuss Geisel stamp, Springfield, MA, October 27, 2003.
3. Judith and Neil Morgan, *Dr. Seuss & Mr. Geisel: A Biography* (New York: Random House, 1995), 276 [CC19950421000].
4. Theodor S. Geisel, "Santy Claus Be Hanged," *Jack-O-Lantern* 17, no. 4 (December 15, 1924): 23 [CC19241215000].
5. Theodor S. Geisel, "Rolling Five into One," *Judge* 99, no. 2565 (December 27, 1930): 10 [CC19301227000].
6. Dr. Seuss, "Greek Origin: The Santaur," *Vanity Fair* 37, no. 4 (December 1931): 68 [CC19311200002].
7. Dr. Seuss, *And to Think That I Saw It on Mulberry Street* (New York: Vanguard Press, 1937), 12 [CC19370900000].
8. Dr. Seuss, "Perfect Present," *Child Life* 32, no. 40 (December 1953): 9 [CC19531200002]. This story was reprinted in *Child Life* (December 1961): 5 [CC19611200000] and Lynne G. Miller, ed., *Ten Tales of Christmas* (Scranton, PA: Scholastic Book Services, 1972), 26 [CC197212z0000].
9. Theodor Seuss Geisel, "Japan's Young Dreams," *Life* 36, no. 13 (March 29, 1954): 89–95 [CC19540329000].
10. Dr. Seuss, "The Kindly Snather," *Redbook* 108, no. 2 (December 1956): 100 [CC19561200001].
11. Phyllis McGinley, "The Year Without a Santa Claus," *Good Housekeeping* 143, no. 6 (December 1956): 95 [CC19561200005].
12. Ibid.
13. Ibid., 96.
14. Ibid., 97.
15. Cynthia Lindsay, "The Miracle of Dr. Seuss," *Good Housekeeping* 151, no. 6 (December 1960): 32–37 [CC19601200001].
16. William B. Hart, "Between the Lines," *Redbook* 110, no. 2 (December 1957): 4 [CC19571200000].
17. George Kane, "And, Dear Dr. Seuss, the Whole World's in Love with Yeuss," *Rocky Mountain News*, February 15, 1976.
18. E. J. Kahn, Jr., "Profiles: Children's Friend," *The New Yorker* 36, no. 44 (December 17, 1960): 84 [CC19601217000].
19. Isobel Ashe, "How a Grinch Stole Christmas: A Yule Video Special," *Newport News Sunday Daily Press* television pullout, December 18, 1966, 2 [CC19661218002].

THE GRINCH

1. Elizabeth Blair, "How the Grinch Stole Christmas," *Morning Edition*, National Public Radio, December 23, 2002 [CC20021223000].
2. *The Oxford English Dictionary*, 1635 citation, "tightly closed, clenched," as cited in Philip Nel, *Dr. Seuss: American Icon* (New York: Continuum, 2004), 25 [CC20040100005].
3. Ibid., 1892 citation, "to make a harsh grating noise," as cited in Nel, *Dr. Seuss: American Icon*, 25 [CC20040100005].
4. *Shorter Oxford English Dictionary*, fifth edition (New York: Oxford University Press, 2002), as cited at www.askoxford.com/worldofwords/wordfrom/shorter/?view=.
5. *Random House Webster's College Dictionary* (New York: Random House, 2000).
6. www.fbi.gov/page2/dec03/fraud120803.htm
7. "[I]n the draft version of 'The Hoobub and the Grinch,' the Grinch was originally called 'Guido'" (Nel, *Dr. Seuss: American Icon*, 118) [CC20040100005].
8. Of course, the look of Ted's Grinch is typical Dr. Seuss. The Grinch and a Zax would be hard to tell apart in a dark alley.
9. George Kane, "And, Dear Dr. Seuss, the Whole World's in Love with Yeuss," *Rocky Mountain News*, February 15, 1976.
10. Hartford Fire Insurance Company advertisement, likely from *The Saturday Evening Post* (1925).
11. Isobel Ashe, "How a Grinch Stole Christmas: A Yule Video Special," *Newport News Sunday Daily Press* television pullout, December 18, 1966, 2 [CC19661218002].
12. Ibid.
13. Ibid.
14. Hal Humphrey, "Special Visit with the Whos," *Los Angeles Times Weekly TV Magazine*, December 18, 1966 [CC19661218001].
15. Judith and Neil Morgan, *Dr. Seuss & Mr. Geisel: A Biography* (New York: Random House, 1995), 189–190 [CC19950421000].
16. According to the press book, production started in September 1965. Other sources cite different dates, ranging from spring 1965 (Ashe, "How a Grinch Stole Christmas") to February 1966 (Humphrey, "Special Visit with the Whos").
17. www.cbs.com/specials/cbs_75/timeline/1960.shtml
18. The early 1960s color programs included *Walt Disney's Wonderful World of Color*, some cartoons, and the first regularly scheduled color program—*Bonanza*. On August 19, 1965, just before production started on *How the Grinch Stole Christmas!* for CBS, *CBS Morning News with Mike Wallace* and *CBS Evening News with Walter Cronkite* became the first regularly scheduled major-network news programs broadcast in color.
19. *A Charlie Brown Christmas* had its debut on CBS on December 9, 1965.
20. www.answers.com/topic/television
21. Dr. Seuss, Emmy Awards acceptance speech, Pasadena, CA, September 17, 1978 [CC19780917000]. Reported in various publications, including *The San Diego Union*, October 15, 1978 [CC19781015000].
22. Dr. Seuss, *The Grinch Grinches the Cat in the Hat* (DePatie-Freleng Enterprises, 1982) [CC19820520020].
23. Ibid.
24. Ibid.
25. *Family Guy*, Episode #5: "A Hero Sits Next Door," premiered May 2, 1999, on Fox. Joe Swanson's fall from the roof in his battle with the Grinch was how he was paralyzed from the waist down.
26. *Johnny Bravo*, Episode #5: "'Twas the Night," premiered August 4, 1997, on the Cartoon Network.
27. *Hang Time*, Episode #76: "Window of Opportunity," premiered November 28, 1998, on NBC.
28. *South Park*, Episode #29: "Merry Christmas Charlie Manson!," premiered December 9, 1998, on Comedy Central. This episode depicted a holiday TV program called *The Grinchiepoo*, by which "Charlie" became distracted.
29. *Tiny Toon Adventures*, Episode #98: "It's a Wonderful Tiny Toon Christmas Special," premiered December 6, 1992, on Fox.
30. *South Park*, Episode #27: "Chef Aid," premiered October 7, 1998, on Comedy Central. The narrator says, "And what happened next? Well, in South Park they say that Johnnie Cochran's small heart grew three sizes that day."
31. *My Life as a Teenage Robot*, Episode #14: "Robot for All Seasons," premiered December 8, 2004, on Nickelodeon. Tucker Carbunkle held a magnifying glass to Todd Sweeney's heart to show how it had grown.
32. *The Venture Brothers*, Episode #15: "A Very Venture Christmas," premiered December 19, 2004, on Cartoon Network. Dr. Venture's heart grew, just like the Grinch's.
33. *Snoops*, Episode #9: "The Grinch," premiered December 12, 1999, on ABC. Gina Gershon's character (Glenn Hall) tried to find out who was stealing Christmas gifts from people's homes.
34. *Frasier*, Episode #57: "Frasier Grinch," premiered December 19, 1995, on NBC.
35. *The X-Files*, Episode #123: "How the Ghosts Stole Christmas," premiered December 13, 1998, on Fox.
36. *Just Shoot Me!*, Episode #41: "How the Finch Stole Christmas," premiered December 15, 1998, on NBC. Dennis Finch sabotaged the magazine office's Christmas party.
37. *ER*, Episode #123: "How the Finch Stole Christmas," premiered December 16, 1999, on NBC. Not to be confused with the identically titled episode of *Just Shoot Me!*, this one referred to Dr. Cleo Finch, played by Michael Michele.
38. *All Grown Up*, Episode #24: "The Finster Who Stole Christmas," premiered December 7, 2004, on Nickelodeon. Chuckie Finster stole a Christmas tree and got the whole town looking for him.
39. *Samurai Pizza Cats*, Episode #47: "The Cheese Who Stole Christmas," premiered November 6, 1990. The Cheese dressed up as Santa Claus to try to ruin Christmas.
40. *Evening Shade*, Episode #11: "The Wood Who Stole Christmas," premiered December 17, 1990, on CBS.
41. *The PJs*, Episode #14: "How the Super Stoled Christmas," premiered December 17, 1999, on Fox. Thurgood Stubbs (voiced by Eddie Murphy) stole tenants' presents.

42. *Nikki,* Episode #9: "The Crybaby Who Stole Christmas," premiered December 17, 2000, on the WB.

43. *The Geena Davis Show,* Episode #10: "The Mom That Stole Christmas," premiered December 19, 2000, on ABC.

44. *Half & Half,* Episode #34: "The Big How the Ex Stole Christmas Episode," premiered December 15, 2003, on UPN.

45. *Beavis and Butt-head,* Episode #56: "A Very Special Christmas with Beavis and Butt-head," premiered December 17, 1993, on MTV.

46. *The Simpsons,* Episode #14: "Bart Gets an F," premiered October 11, 1990, on Fox.

47. *House,* Episode #23: "Acceptance," premiered September 13, 2005, on Fox.

48. *The Pretender,* Episode #8: "Not Even a Mouse," premiered December 14, 1996, on NBC. While Jarod investigated the death of a homeless man and tried to identify a Jane Doe before Christmas, Miss Parker told someone who was worried about Jarod, "Relax. He's probably holed up in Who-ville, experiencing the Grinch for the first time."

49. *King of the Hill,* Episode #4: "Hank's Got the Willies," premiered February 9, 1997, on Fox. Hank Hill told Bill Dauterive that "Santa Claus is for babies," and Bill responded, "You're a mean one, Mr. Grinch."

50. *That '70s Show,* Episode #12: "The Best Christmas Ever," premiered December 13, 1998, on Fox. The main group of high school friends was watching *How the Grinch Stole Christmas!* when Donna Pinciotti, played by Laura Prepon, declared, "Man, the Grinch has a big butt!"

51. *Buffy the Vampire Slayer,* Episode #44: "Amends," premiered December 15, 1998, on the WB. A reference is made to "roast beast," the traditional Who Christmas dinner fare.

52. *Made in Canada,* Episode #16: "The Christmas Show," premiered December 6, 1999, on CBC (Canadian Broadcasting Corporation). Alan Roy was in a bad mood, so he canceled Christmas at the office, causing the staff to nickname him "the Grinch."

53. *Buzz Lightyear of Star Command,* Episode #59: "Holiday Time," premiered December 16, 2000, on the Family Channel. This episode relied on the Dr. Seuss story as the basis for Evil Emperor Zurg's stealing Christmas.

54. *Lizzie McGuire,* Episode #51: "Xtreme Xmas," premiered December 6, 2002, on the Disney Channel. Matt McGuire called his older sister a Grinch.

55. *Committed,* Episode #6: "The Birthday Episode," premiered January 25, 2005, on NBC. Marni Fliss's boyfriend, Nate Solomon, said of her exuberantly decorated apartment, "It's Christmas in Who-ville over there!"

56. *South Park,* Episode #71: "Cartmanland," premiered July 25, 2001, on Comedy Central.

In the Chuck Jones version of *How the Grinch Stole Christmas!,* the Grinch told Max:

> For tomorrow, I know,
> All those *Who* girls and boys
> Will wake bright and early,
> They'll rush for their toys,
> And then—oh the noise,
> Oh the noise, noise, noise, noise!
> If there's one thing I hate—
> All the noise, noise, noise, noise!

The Grinch's pupils spun within his eyes as he thought about the instruments on which the Whos would make a racket.

In a direct parody, Cartman said of theme parks, "The rides are great, but all the lines, lines, lines! If there's one thing I hate—all the lines, lines, lines, lines. . . ." Then his pupils spun as he slipped into Seussian rhyme and continued in Grinchly fashion:

> Then there's lines for the bathrooms,
> Lines for the drinks,
> Lines for kantankers
> And rare kartankula plinks.

The character blowing the kantanker is an homage to the Who blowing a Floo Floober and banging a Tah Tinker in the cartoon version of *How the Grinch Stole Christmas!*

57. *The Simpsons,* Episode #76: "Last Exit to Springfield," premiered March 11, 1993, on Fox. With Homer Simpson acting as his union's negotiator, his boss, Mr. Burns, said, "They sing without juicers, they sing without blenders. They sing without flunjers, capdabblers, and smendlers."

58. *The Simpsons,* Episode #256: "Skinner's Sense of Snow," premiered December 17, 2000, on Fox. Principal Skinner told snowed-in students, "We're going to watch my favorite movie about a grinchy little character who tries to steal Christmas."

59. *The Simpsons,* Episode #320: "'Tis the Fifteenth Season," premiered December 14, 2003, on Fox. Homer was heard singing a parody of "You're a Mean One, Mr. Grinch" while sneaking into people's homes.

60. Attorney Michael Lynn's "How the Grinch Stole Christmas Vacation" (December 20, 2004) has been available at www.snopes.com/legal/graphics/grinch.pdf. Lynn (of the law firm Lynn Tillotson & Pinker) represented plaintiffs Jenkens & Gilchrist and L. Steven Leshin. Alfonso Garcia Chan (of Akin, Gump, Strauss, Hauer & Feld) represented defendants Stuart D. Dwork and Roger Maxwell. An explanation of the conflict that prompted the parody has been available at www.snopes.com/holidays/christmas/humor/grinch.asp.

61. Compare the November 2000 parody "How the Grinch Stole the Election," presented by Bill Maher on the television show *Politically Incorrect* (previously available at www.seuss.org/seuss/pi-grinch.html) with the December 2000 parody "How Al Sore Stole the Election by Dr. Ruse," penned by Nancy Renko (previously available at www.seuss.org/seuss/alsore.html).

62. Rob Suggs, "The Binch," September 13, 2001 [CC20010913000]. This piece has been available at http://media.radcity.net/KILT/thebinch.txt, although Mr. Suggs's publisher, InterVarsity Press, has apparently been pursuing a copyright to protect the work.

63. Kevin Horrigan, "How the Liberals Stole Christmas (or) A Visit from St. Dick," *St. Louis Post-Dispatch,* December 11, 2005.

64. Bill Press, *How the Republicans Stole Christmas: The Republican Party's Declared Monopoly on Religion and What Democrats Can Do to Take It Back* (New York: Doubleday Books, 2005).

65. Randy Singer, *The Judge Who Stole Christmas* (New York: WaterBrook Press, 2005).

MAX

1. Judith and Neil Morgan, *Dr. Seuss & Mr. Geisel: A Biography* (New York: Random House, 1995), 30 [CC19950421000].

2. Theodor S. Geisel, "The Dachs-Deer," *Judge* 93, no. 2406 (December 10, 1927): 15 [CC19271210000].

3. Frankie Kowalski, "How the Grinch Stole Christmas . . . and My Heart," *Animation World Magazine* 1, no. 9 (December 1996) [CC19961200000]. Kowalski quotes Chuck Jones at a benefit for the Motion Picture & Television Fund in Newport Beach, CA.

4. Dr. Seuss, "Max's Song (What Am I Doing Here?)," *Halloween Is Grinch Night* (DePatie-Freleng Enterprises, 1977) [CC19771028000].

THE WHOS

1. Jonathan Cott, "The Good Dr. Seuss," in *Pipers at the Gates of Dawn: The Wisdom of Children's Literature* (New York: Random House, 1983), 19 [CC19830400000].

2. Edward Connery Lathem, "Words and Pictures Married: The Beginnings of Dr. Seuss . . . ," *Dartmouth Alumni Magazine* (April 1976): 18 [CC19760400000].

3. Judith and Neil Morgan, *Dr. Seuss & Mr. Geisel: A Biography* (New York: Random House, 1995), 53–54 [CC19950421000].

4. Lathem, "Words and Pictures Married," 18 [CC19760400000].

5. Morgan, *Dr. Seuss & Mr. Geisel,* 238 [CC19950421000].

6. Robert Cahn, "The Wonderful World of Dr. Seuss," *The Saturday Evening Post* 230, no. 1 (July 6, 1957): 46 [CC19570706000].

7. Ruth K. MacDonald, *Dr. Seuss* (Boston: Twayne Publishers, 1988), 97 [CC19881201000].

8. Leslie Raddatz, "Dr. Seuss Climbs Down from His Mountain to Bring the Grinch to Television," *TV Guide,* Chicago metropolitan edition, December 17, 1966, 14 [CC19661217000].

9. Theodor S. Geisel, *How the Grinch Stole Christmas!* recording scripts (draft notes and corrections), Mandeville Special Collections Library, Geisel Library, University of California, San Diego, MSS 0230, Box 14, Folder 11. In many pages of draft notes and corrections for the script of the Chuck Jones production, Ted created dialogue for the Whos. He eventually scrapped that idea, but many of Ted's working lyrics for the song "Welcome, Christmas" were based on this Who language.

10. Digby Diehl, "Q & A: 'Dr. Seuss,'" *Los Angeles Times WEST Magazine,* September 17, 1972, 39 [CC19720917000].

11. Diane Roback, "Coming Attractions: Several Notable Authors and Artists Discuss Their Current Projects," *Publishers Weekly* 237, no. 8 (February 23, 1990): 126 [CC19900223000].

12. Glenn Edward Sadler, "Maurice Sendak and Dr. Seuss: A Conversation," *The Horn Book Magazine* 65, no. 5 (September/October 1989): 586 [CC19890900000].

13. Diehl, "Q & A: 'Dr. Seuss,'" 39 [CC19720917000].

14. Ted routinely reported that it took him three months to finish the entire book. Of course, in typical Ted fashion, he also said, "I spent three months on the last page of 'The Grinch.' It kept turning into a religious tract." (George Kane, "And, Dear Dr. Seuss, the Whole World's in Love with Yeuss," *Rocky Mountain News* [February 15, 1976].)

CHRISTMAS AND DR. SEUSS

p. 54, *How the Grinch Stole Christmas!* Junior Literary Guild edition (New York: Random House, 1957), cover [CC19571000001].

p. 54, *Thegar Trölli stal jólunum* (Reykjavík: Mál og Menning, 2001), cover [CC19571000075/2001].

p. 54, *Como o Grinch Roubou o Natal* (São Paulo: Editora Schwarcz LTDA, 2000), cover [CC19571000070/200012].

p. 54, *Wie der Grinch Weihnachten gestohlen hat!* (Munich: Piper Verlag GmbH, 2002), cover [CC19571000056/2000].

p. 55, *Il Grinch* (Milan: Arnoldo Mondadori, 2000), cover [CC19571000068/200011].

p. 55, *Hogyan lopta el a Görcs a karácsonyt* (Budapest: Arktisz Kiadó, 2000), cover [CC19571000062/2000].

p. 55, *Gurinichi* (Tokyo: Atisuto Hausu, 2000), cover [CC19571000064/200011].

p. 55, *Comment le grinch a volé Noël* (Paris: Pocket Jeunesse, 2000), cover [CC19571000063/200011].

p. 56, Dr. Seuss, "Greek Origin: The Santaur," *Vanity Fair* 37, no. 4 (December 1931): 68 [CC19311200002].

p. 56, Dr. Seuss, "Rolling Five into One," *Judge* 99, no. 2565 (December 27, 1930): 10 [CC19301227000].

p. 56, Dr. Seuss, Christmas card: "Apparently, there IS a Santa Claus!" (circa 1935) [CC1935z12000].

p. 56, Dr. Seuss, Christmas card: "After all, Reindeer are SO Common!" (December 1936) [CC19361200010].

p. 57, Dr. Seuss, "Perfect Present," *Child Life* 32, no. 40 (December 1953): 9 [CC19531200002].

p. 58, Dr. Seuss, "A Prayer for a Child," *Collier's* 136, no. 13 (December 23, 1955): 86 [CC19551223000].

p. 60, *Redbook* 110, no. 2 (December 1957): 4, "Seuss looking like a Grinch" [CC19571200000].

THE GRINCH

p. 63, Dr. Seuss, *How the Grinch Stole Christmas!* (New York: Random House, 1957), 12, "Then he got an idea!" [CC19571000000].

p. 64, Dr. Seuss, "The Hoobub and the Grinch," *Redbook* 105, no. 1 (May 1955): 19 [CC19550500000].

p. 64, Dr. Seuss, *Scrambled Eggs Super!* (New York: Random House, 1953), 11, image of the Beagle-Beaked-Bald-Headed Grinch [CC19530312000].

p. 65, Dr. Seuss, Holly Sugar advertisement, presentation cel (circa July 1955), image of Grinch-like character [CC195507z0001].

p. 65, Dr. Seuss, *How the Grinch Stole Christmas!* (New York: Random House, 1957), 47, "And the Grinch, with his grinch-feet ice-cold in the snow . . ." [CC19571000000].

p. 65, advertisement: Hartford Fire Insurance Company, probably *The Saturday Evening Post* (1925).

p. 66, photograph: Ted Geisel and Chuck Jones (July 1966), CBS/Landov.

p. 67, Dr. Seuss, *How the Grinch Stole Christmas!* (New York: Random House, 1957), 2, Grinch in repose by cave [CC19571000000].

p. 67, *TV Guide* (Chicago Metropolitan Edition) 14, no. 51 (December 17, 1966): 12, Grinch in repose (from Metro-Goldwyn-Mayer, Inc.). Image used with permission of Turner Entertainment Co. A Time Warner Company. *How the Grinch Stole Christmas* © Turner Entertainment Co. A Time Warner Company. All rights reserved.

p. 68, *Halloween Is Grinch Night* production cel, Seq 16 Sc 1 G 3 (DePatie-Freleng Enterprises, 1977), 4:22 into movie, image of Grinch puzzling just before saying, "It's a wonderful night for eyebrows" [CC19771029011].

p. 68, *Halloween Is Grinch Night* VHS box-cover detail (Farmington Hills, MI: CBS/Fox Playhouse Video, 1985), image of Grinch looking up while holding rod [CC19771029100/1985].

p. 69, *Halloween Is Grinch Night* promotional still photograph (ABC Television Press Relations, October 1977), "The always obedient Max must suffer the cruelties of his master, the evil Grinch, although he longs to be a happy puppy once again, in the ABC Holiday special 'Halloween Is Grinch Night' to be aired on the ABC Television Network SATURDAY, OCTOBER 29 (8:00–8:30 p.m., EDT)" [CC19771004005].

p. 69, *The Grinch Grinches the Cat in the Hat* production cel, MP 4002 5 G57 (DePatie-Freleng Enterprises, 1982), 0:04 into movie, image of Grinch yawning upon waking [CC19820520013].

p. 70, *The Grinch Grinches the Cat in the Hat* production cel (DePatie-Freleng Enterprises, 1982), 6:12 into movie, image of Grinch with hot dog, yelling, "Greenface?!" [CC19820520020].

p. 71, *The Grinch Grinches the Cat in the Hat* production sketch (DePatie-Freleng Enterprises, 1982), 23:08 into movie, image of Grinch's mother as she says, "Yes, son. Now be a good boy and clean up your room" [CC19820520050].

MAX

p. 73, Dr. Seuss, *How the Grinch Stole Christmas!* (New York: Random House, 1957), 42, image of Max with antlers tied on head [CC19571000000].

p. 73, Dr. Seuss, "The Dachs-Deer," *Judge* 93, no. 2406 (December 10, 1927): 15 [CC19271210000].

p. 73, Dr. Seuss, original sketch of the Dax-Deer (circa 1960s) [CC196z0000000].

p. 73, Dr. Seuss, "1,647,829 B.C. Experiments between reindeer and dachshund result in fiasco," *Life* 101, no. 2587 (February 1934): 22 [CC19340200000].

p. 74, Steven Mfg. Co. Dachsheer [CC19720000102].

p. 74, Dr. Seuss, *How the Grinch Stole Christmas!* (New York: Random House, 1957), 36–37, image of Max pulling sled up Mt. Crumpit [CC19571000000].

p. 74, *Halloween Is Grinch Night* promotional still photograph (ABC Television Press Relations, October 1977), image of Max pulling the Grinch aboard the Paraphernalia Wagon [CC19771004010].

p. 75, publicity still: Grinch looking at Max, who is hanging from rope. (*How the Grinch Stole Christmas* © Turner Entertainment Co. A Time Warner Company. All Rights Reserved.) (1966)

p. 75, *The Grinch Grinches the Cat in the Hat* VHS box-cover detail (Farmington Hills, MI: CBS/Fox Playhouse Video, 1985), image of the Grinch holding Max by his collar [CC19820520010B/1985z].

p. 75, *The Grinch Grinches the Cat in the Hat* production cel, 4002 299A T-5 (DePatie-Freleng Enterprises, 1982), 23:52 into movie, image of Max winking after setting the Acoustical Anti-Audial Bleeper (Vacu-Sound-Sweeper) on the Grinch's mirror reflection [CC19820520057].

THE WHOS

p. 76, Dr. Seuss, *How the Grinch Stole Christmas!* (New York: Random House, 1957), 1, image of Who with wreath [CC19571000000].

p. 76, Palmer Cox, *The Brownies: Their Book* (New York: Appleton-Century-Crofts, Inc., 1887), 19, image of Brownie holding bicycle tire [CC1887000000/1915].

p. 77, Dr. Seuss, *Horton Hears a Who!* (New York: Random House, 1954), 7, "some poor little person who's shaking with fear" [CC19540812000].

p. 77, Dr. Seuss, detail from Flit advertisement: "Now you young scamps behave yourselves—or you'll wake up on Christmas and find your stockings full of Flit," *Life* 96, no. 2509 (December 5, 1930): 52 [CC19301205000].

p. 77, Dr. Seuss, *How the Grinch Stole Christmas!* (New York: Random House, 1957), 50, detail from illustration of "*The Grinch carved the roast beast!*" [CC19571000000].

p. 77, Dr. Seuss, "Sex laws are illogical: The Patagonian Hepatica (magnified 800 times) can become a father at the age of three minutes," *Life* 101, no. 2589 (April 1934): 28 [CC19340400000].

p. 77, Dr. Seuss, *The Saturday Evening Post* 213, no. 47 (May 24, 1941): inside rear cover, advertisement: Dupont Cellophane [CC19410524000].

p. 77, Dr. Seuss, *Horton Hears a Who!* (New York: Random House, 1954), 35, "Will you stick by us *Whos* while we're making repairs?" [CC19540812000].

p. 78, Dr. Seuss, *Horton Hears a Who!* (New York: Random House, 1954), 43, detail of Who on flower [CC19540812000].

p. 78, Dr. Seuss, Stromberg-Carlson "What Is a Wild Tone?" advertising booklet (circa 1932), 03, detail of Wild Tone yelling [CC19370000000].

p. 78, Dr. Seuss, Stromberg-Carlson "What Is a Wild Tone?" advertising booklet (circa 1932), 05, detail of Wild Tone banging drum [CC19370000000].

p. 78, Dr. Seuss, *How the Grinch Stole Christmas!* (New York: Random House, 1957), 7, detail of Who with drum [CC19571000000].

p. 79, *How the Grinch Stole Christmas!* production cel (Metro-Goldwyn-Mayer, Inc., 1966), 4:06 into movie, "They'll blow their Floo Floobers, they'll bang their Tah Tinkers . . ." [CC19661218022]. This image was reused as a *Horton Hears a Who!* production cel (Metro-Goldwyn-Mayer, Inc., 1966), 19:56 into movie, "Play on a pizzer . . ." [CC19700319105]. Image used with permission of Turner Entertainment Co. A Time Warner Company. *How the Grinch Stole Christmas* © Turner Entertainment Co. A Time Warner Company. All rights reserved.

p. 79, Dr. Seuss, *How the Grinch Stole Christmas!* (New York: Random House, 1957), 29, image of Cindy-Lou Who looking at Grinch stealing tree [CC19571000000].

p. 79, publicity still: Cindy-Lou Who holding an ornament. (*How the Grinch Stole Christmas* © Turner Entertainment Co. A Time Warner Company. All Rights Reserved.) (1966)

p. 79, *Halloween Is Grinch Night* VHS box-cover detail (Farmington Hills, MI: CBS/Fox Playhouse Video, 1985), image of Ukariah Who [CC19771029100/1985].

p. 82, photograph: Ted Geisel (July 1966), CBS/Landov.